COUPONS FOR FREE STUFF

JUST CUT THEM OUT AND USE THEM WHENEVER YOU'RE SHORT ON **CASH**

UPON PRESENTATION OF THIS COUPON, YOU MUST

SHUT UP.

AND STAY SHUTTED-UP FOR ONE FULL **HOUR**

Okay, technically this won't help your cash situation but it's still good.

THINK YOU CAN HANDLE JAMIE KELLY'S FIRST YEAR OF DIARIES?

#1 LET'S PRETEND THIS NEVER HAPPENED

#2 MY PANTS ARE HAUNTED!

#3 AM I THE PRINCESS OR THE FROG?

#4 NEVER DO ANYTHING, EVER

#5 CAN ADULTS BECOME HUMAN?

#6 THE PROBLEM WITH HERE IS THAT IT'S WHERE I'M FROM

#7 NEVER UNDERESTIMATE YOUR DUMBNESS

#8 IT'S NOT MY FAULT I KNOW EVERYTHING

#9 THAT'S WHAT FRIENDS AREN'T FOR

#10 THE WORST THINGS IN LIFE ARE ALSO FREE

#11 OKAY, SO MAYBE I DO HAVE SUPERPOWERS

#12 ME! (JUST LIKE YOU, ONLY BETTER)

AND DON'T MISS YEAR TWO!

YEAR TWO #1: SCHOOL. HASN'T THIS GONE ON LONG ENOUGH?

YEAR TWO #2: THE SUPER-NICE ARE SUPER-ANNOYING

YEAR TWO #3: NOBODY'S PERFECT. I'M AS CLOSE AS IT GETS.

YEAR TWO #4: WHAT I DON'T KNOW MIGHT HURT ME

Jim Benton's Tales from Mackerel Middle School

DEAR DUMB DIARY,

THE WORST THINGS IN LIFE ARE ALSO FREE

BY JAMIE KELLY

SCHOLASTIC INC.

ISBN 978-0-545-11614-5

20 19 18 17 17 18 19 20/0

Printed in the U.S.A. 40

First printing, June 2010

For Janet, Jerry, Patrick, and Kristin

Special thanks to Kristen LeClerc and the team at Scholastic: Steve Scott, Elizabeth Krych, Susan Jeffers, Anna Bloom, and Shannon Penney.

THIS DIARY IS PROPERTY OF

Jamie Kelly

FAVORITE VACATION: Summer

FAVORITE PLACE TO GO ON VACATION: Amusement Parks But not if they have clowns

FAVORITE KIND OF MONEY: Money? what's money??

DO NOT READ MY DIARY OR I SWEAR if I **EVER** FIND A Genie, I will ask him to MAKE ALL of your Money DISAPPEAR!

And if you don't have any money, first I'll ask him to give you a JILLION DOLLARS

and then

TAKE IT AWAY!!

Dear Whoever Is Reading My Dumb Diary,

So I suppose you think it's okay to just pick up somebody's diary and read it absolutely free of charge?

Well, it **isn't**. Things cost money in this world, cupcake, and if you want to read this diary, it's going to cost you. Have a look at our handy price list:

HOW MUCH IT COSTS TO READ JAMIE'S DIARY:

People: Five million dollars
Parents: Four million dollars (apiece)
Isabella: One million dollars (non-counterfeit, and no offense, Isabella, but I'll need to have somebody at the bank check it out first)
Blond individuals: One arm and one leg. Plus five million dollars. Plus another five million dollars.

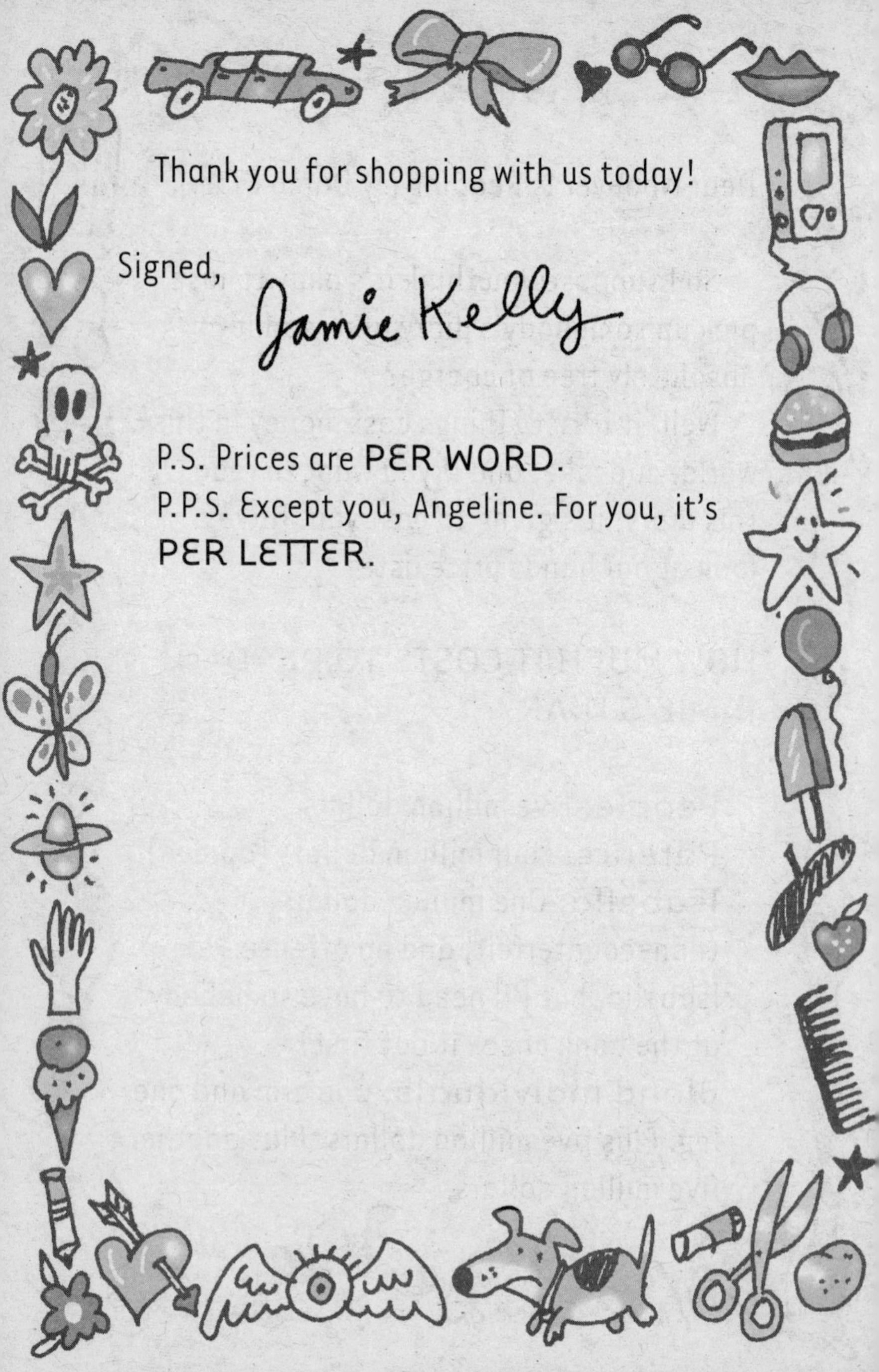

Thank you for shopping with us today!

Signed,

Jamie Kelly

P.S. Prices are **PER WORD**.

P.P.S. Except you, Angeline. For you, it's **PER LETTER**.

Sunday 01

Dear Dumb Diary,

Sometimes teachers think it's okay to teach things to kids, and they are proven wrong. Like a little earlier this year, in science, when we were each assigned a disease to study. The diseases were written on little slips of paper, and we chose them by grabbing them at random out of a bag.

Angeline, of course, unfairly got the **BUBONIC PLAGUE**, which is like the most popular disease **EVER**. I was assigned **SUNBURN**, which I complained wasn't even really a disease. I asked for **DIAPER RASH** instead because that's sort of the cutest disease, but then the teacher said no and that I'd just have to pull another one at random out of a bag. I was afraid I might get **FAT BUTT** or something like that, although now that I think about it, I'm not sure that Fat Buttedness is a medical condition. Anyway, I decided to just shut up and live with sunburn.

Angeline offered to give me the plague, but I didn't want anybody's charity, you know?

The **REAL** problem here was that Isabella picked this condition called *neurapraxia*, which is not as famous as the bubonic plague, but believe me — more people have had it. Neurapraxia is the scientific name for that tingle when your arm or leg falls asleep. It does not have the horrible and gory symptoms that Isabella had hoped for (I can't remember them all because Isabella was laughing too hard while she was listing them), but Isabella seemed satisfied that left untreated, neurapraxia could become the kind of illness she could love.

So we all researched our diseases, and finally the day came when some of us were supposed to stand in front of the class and bore each other with our reports. We had a substitute the day Isabella was scheduled to give her report. I know that teachers think it's okay to be absent sometimes, but they are **wrong** about that, too.

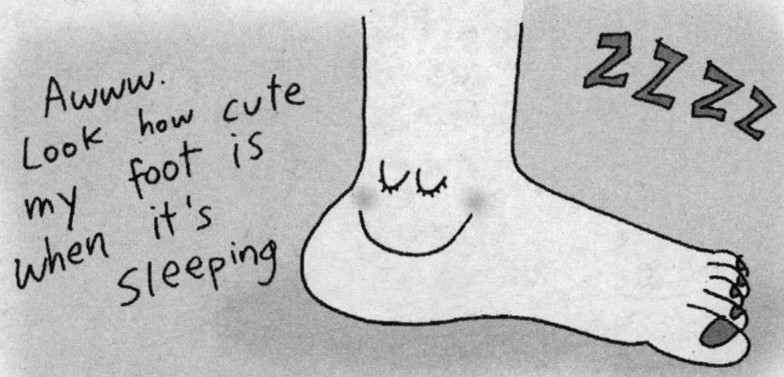

Isabella stood up and began slowly and carefully describing neurapraxia, and how standing up and moving the limb seems to clear it up. But then she began to talk about various other gross things that could happen to you if your neurapraxia went on too long, and you couldn't get the symptoms to go away, or if you got it in your brain, maybe from a tight hat, or a pillow that was too soft or too warm or not soft enough. And believe me: Isabella is very fluent in gross. She can stretch the word "pus" into three syllables.

About five minutes into her report, just as everybody was totally sick to their stomachs, Isabella pulled out a test tube that she took from the lab where her dad works. She said that they had discovered a *contagious* form of neurapraxia and that what she had was a REAL TEST TUBE full of it.

The substitute teacher thought Isabella was joking, and didn't think it was a funny joke at that. She told Isabella to put the tube back in her backpack. Teachers also think it's okay to assume that Isabella is always just joking about things, and they are **wrong** about this as well. She isn't always joking.

When Isabella went to reach for her bag, she accidentally dropped the tube and it broke open. I've never seen Isabella look so frightened. In just a couple seconds, she started to twitch and foam dribbled out of her mouth.

By the time Isabella hit the floor, Mike Pinsetti was in a **full shrieking panic**, running into the halls and screaming, "EVACUATE THE SCHOOL! EVACUATE THE SCHOOL!"

This got the whole class freaked out and everyone ran out of the room, because, frankly, nobody is really sure what Isabella is capable of. Other teachers, hearing Pinsetti's shrill feminine screams, assumed it was coming from the mouth of a woman (like a teacher) and did the safe thing — they marched the kids out of the school. They kind of have to do this, because I think their pay depends on how many kids are alive at the end of each school year.

Angeline and I know that Isabella's dad doesn't work in a lab, and we've seen Isabella dribble foam from her mouth before. So when the ambulance guys and police officers came in about forty-five minutes later, they found me and Angeline and Isabella in the classroom playing cards.

By that time, Isabella had wiped the saliva froth off her chin, but they still didn't believe her when she tried to convince them that I was Isabella. She's a masterful liar, but Isabella is not unknown to the police.

Then she explained what happened. She told the police that the teacher gave us a disease assignment. It was supposed to have visual aids, and we were supposed to **dramatically communicate** just how our disease works. Isabella said she tried to talk our teacher out of it, since she feared this exact thing might happen — Isabella is just so naturally good at convincing people of things like diseases. Isabella told them that our substitute teacher was stubborn and insisted we do it this way, and that she also said a lot of suspicious things that struck Isabella as being very anti-cop.

Angeline and I nodded in agreement as Isabella talked. Not agreement to the anti-cop part, or even the tried-to-talk-her-out-of-it part. Also not the visual aids or dramatically communicating part. We were nodding in agreement that Mrs. Palmer, the science teacher, had given us an assignment.

Of course, by that time they had evacuated the school as a precaution, and sent everyone home. That would have been great except for one thing: If your school loses too many days during the year, like for weather, or power outages, or fake neurapraxia-C outbreaks, you have to make it up at the end of the year. Isabella put us one day over the line. So even though the **last day of school** was supposed to be Friday, now it's tomorrow.

(Oh, by the way, this is neat. I saw that substitute last week. She mows lawns for a living now. And she looks a lot happier than she did back when she was a sub and was running out of the school.)

what she was probably thinking

Monday 02

Dear Dumb Diary,

It's finally **the last day of school!** I always think that nobody in the whole world could be any happier than I am about it, but then I see grins on the faces of teachers that I didn't think even had grin muscles.

I used to wonder why teachers were the only adults that got three-month vacations, but now I know it's because they're the only adults that deserve them. They probably don't do cool things like hang out at the beach, though. I think they spend the full three months in an insane asylum to prepare for the next year. That's why you never see teachers looking all teachery at amusement parks or the beach or anything. They're locked up somewhere, taking special tests with number two pencils.

We had a little end-of-the-year party today. It was one of those healthy-type parties, so they served beautiful and delicious fruits and vegetables for us to reject.

We also had to clean out our lockers. I don't know exactly how much a locker is supposed to hold, but I know this — it can hold **even more** than that.

I had clothes in there that are no longer in fashion, a bottle of Platinum Aqua glitter — please, nobody at my level uses that color anymore — and then I found a peach. I remembered exactly where it was from.

Many, many diaries ago, there was an incident involving a peach rolling out of my lunch bag. Mike Pinsetti attemped to nickname me **"Peach Girl"** as a result. I have no idea why he thought that was a clever nickname, but nicknames can be pretty horrible unless you invent them for yourself, like I'm pretty sure **Captain Excellent** might have done — although he insists he didn't.

At the time, I just grabbed the peach and stuck it back in my lunch bag. It sat in its brown, papery tomb until today, when I pulled it out.

Note to self: ***NEVER*** determine the contents of an old lunch bag by sticking your nose into it and sniffing. Here's why: Right after I did, Hudson walked past and I wanted to say, "Hey, Hudson, big plans for the summer?" But what I actually said was, "Hey, Hudtin, bib pan por duh tummah?" Then I had to stand there listening to his reply ***with my nostrils full of the fruit flies I had inhaled a few moments earlier.*** I was faced with this horrible choice: **BLOW BUGS OUT OF MY NOSE** in front of the eighth-cutest boy in my grade, or snurf them up so deep in my sinuses that they could never, ever escape.

Isabella, being my best friend in the world, decided to cover for me and/or rob me by quickly swooping in and grabbing the bag out of my hand. She caused enough of a distraction for me to secretly blow my nose on a social studies report I had spent two weeks writing. (Sorry, People of Australia.)

Isabella pulled out the peach and held it up in her hand: a stinky, gray, withered little sphere with dents and creases and patches of fuzz here and there.

"I love this," she said in a passionate whisper. "Can I have it?"

"Yeds, fide," I said, still a bit congested from my infestation. "Tage it. Ids all yours. You dode hab to share it wid eddybody."

Isabella waggled the peachish thing in Hudson's face. **"All mine,"** she said.

It's always such a joy walking out of school at the end of the year — no more homework, no more school lunches, no more boredom.

Here are just **some** of the things I'm going to do this summer.

Become famous for great acts of vegetarianism

Swim with dolphins. Or koalas – don't care.

Ride a rollercoaster (with way less barf this time)

Watch every scary movie ever made and get whatever extensive therapy is neccesary afterwards

melt 1000 popsicles.

Re-freeze them into one MASSIVE Popsicle.

Tuesday 03

Dear Dumb Diary,

Okay, I couldn't sleep in today. I tried, but I think school programmed me to wake up at a certain time because I've been doing it all year. Tomorrow I'll sleep in, you'll see. I'll sleep in until noon or 1:00 p.m. Maybe I won't even get out of bed all day. It will be like I'm this girl who just luxuriates in bed all day because she is fabulously wealthy or horribly ill. It will be great.

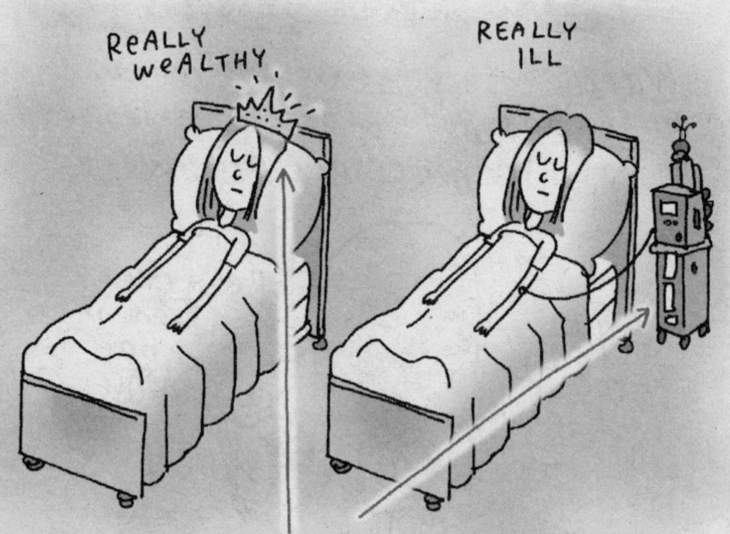

I had planned to become a vegetarian this summer, but Dad made bacon this morning, so I decided to become a vegetarian by lunchtime. That also didn't work out, because Mom and I got hamburgers at the drive-thru.

I think a lot of people, like me, love animals in both ways — with all of our hearts, and with all of our teeth as well. It's just so difficult not to eat their adorable little delicious bodies.

I'll bet I could run a very successful farm by just raising **mean, cranky** animals that nobody would mind eating. It would be like: "Would you like to try the T-bone steak tonight? He trampled four children one day." "Oh yes, that sounds delicious. And for an appetizer, I wonder if you have any chicken wings from birds that tried to peck somebody in the face?"

At dinner tonight, I talked a little about my summer plans. Mom and Dad made their "expensive" face at every one of my ideas. I don't know how they do it, but they have a way of tilting their heads and twisting their eyebrows as if to say, "That Costs Too Much," without ever actually opening their mouths. It's like living with a pair of disapproving mimes.

I called Isabella after dinner and asked her to make a list of her summer plans and bring it over tomorrow, so we could see whose list is better. I had to caution her because her list last year had a couple things on it that I think are illegal to even put on a list. Isabella says that if you write "just kidding" after anything you write, you can't be held accountable for it.

I'm not sure that would always work.

I've stayed up really, really late tonight so that I'll sleep in tomorrow. I'm sure I have the **strength, ambition, and willpower** to lie in bed like a worthless piece of garbage till noon.

Oh, and in case you're wondering, Dumb Diary, my vegetarianism didn't work out at dinner, either. Dad brought home a pepperoni pizza. But I choose to believe that the pepperoni was made from a pig that donated his body to science.

(I know that pizzas aren't exactly science, but I bet scientists eat a lot of pizza, and pizzas need pepperonis, and anyway, shut up.)

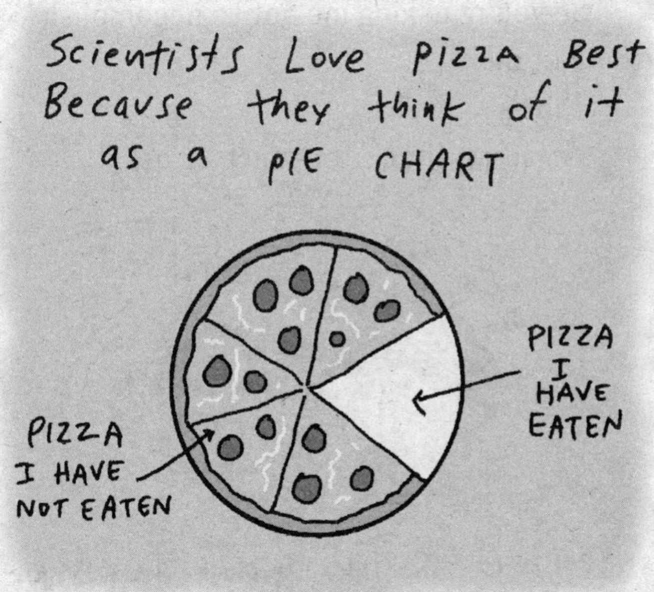

Scientists Love Pizza Best Because they think of it as a PIE CHART

PIZZA I HAVE EATEN

PIZZA I HAVE NOT EATEN

Wednesday 04

Dear Dumb Diary,

I woke up at exactly the same time this morning as when I was using my alarm clock. I lay there for a looong time, trying to fall back asleep. Wouldn't you think that falling asleep is the easiest thing a person could do? It's like the total opposite of doing something hard:

"We want you to just lie there and not do anything. Don't think or talk, either."

"So you're asking me not to accomplish anything at all?"

"That's right."

"I'm sorry, that's too much to ask."

Isabella came over at lunch. We had a vegetarian lunch of grilled cheese sandwiches, which my mom didn't ruin because Isabella made them. Isabella's mom is an incredible cook, so Isabella must have inherited her mother's instincts for making cheese sandwiches in the way cows inherit the instinct to make cheese.

I know what you're thinking, Dumb Diary: Some vegetarians don't eat cheese. Those are called **vegans**. But I can't be that. I'm the kind of vegetarian that *does* eat cheese and some meat but not meat for every single meal every single day. So for certain temporary periods of time I'm a vegetarian. I think maybe I'm a **vegetempian**.

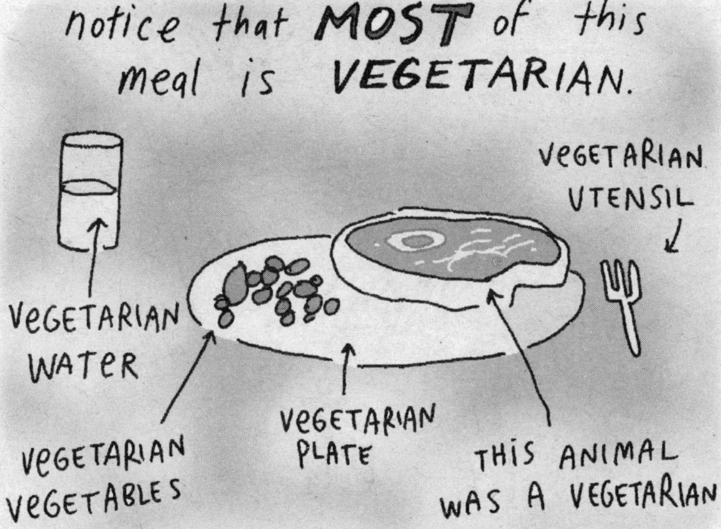

One of my all-time favorite things to do in the summer is go to the zoo, but Isabella refuses to go anymore because of the warthog.

A warthog, Dumb Diary, is a pig that didn't feel it was ugly enough just being a pig, so it went the extra distance and became smaller, and wartier, with a knobby face and tusks and a scraggly mane and very unpleasant attitude.

The warthog at our zoo is named **Loverboy.** It's Isabella's favorite animal, and always has been. When we were little and went to the zoo, she would run all the way to the warthog's enclosure.

But Loverboy is old now, and he never wants to come out of his little cave because they say the sun bothers him. So now we can't go to the zoo because Isabella won't go unless she can see the warthog, and everybody knows it.

But I got her to make a list of things that she *does* want to do this summer. You'll notice that many of these are in no way illegal.

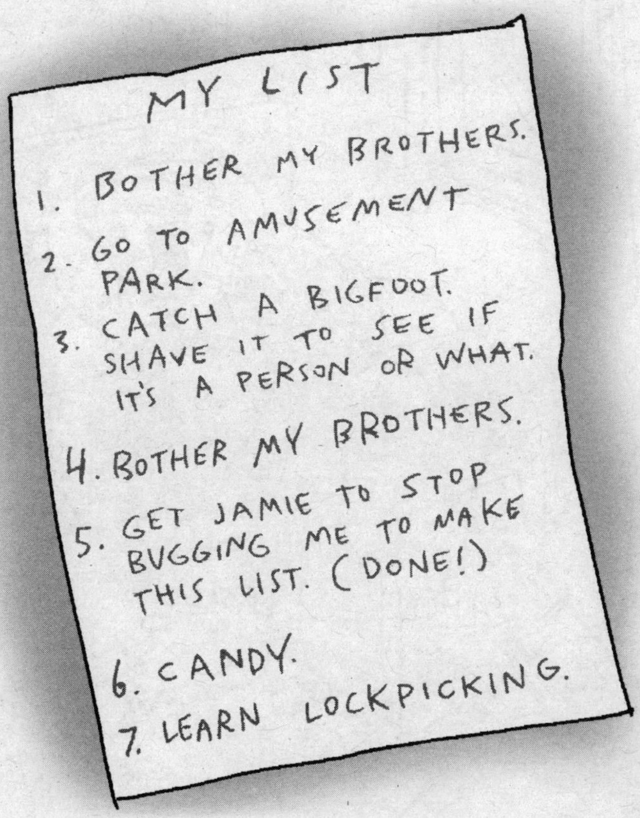

Tomorrow, we plan to get started doing things on the list. I told Isabella I'd call her when I woke up, which is going to be right around noon.

Thursday 05

Dear Dumb Diary,

I woke up even earlier today than I usually do. Stinker and Stinkette were fast asleep; my parents were fast asleep; the rest of the world was fast asleep except for people that unwisely chose jobs that make you get up early, like policemen. Now that I think about it, that must mean crooks get up really early, too. Otherwise, why would the police be up? Strange. Crooks strike me as the type that would **sleep in**.

They say the early bird gets the worm — they never said that he *pays* for it.

My mom dropped me off at Isabella's today. We hung around outside most of the time because her mean older brothers were inside playing video games and, according to Isabella, plotting some sort of horrible scheme against her and trying on pretty dresses.

They weren't *really* trying on pretty dresses. Isabella just likes to yell that loud enough for the neighbors to hear. She goes out of her way to make her brothers unhappy. She often asks herself, "What would make my brothers unhappy?" So she won't forget, she sometimes wears a bracelet that she made with the letters WWMMBU on it.

As we reviewed our List of Summer Excellence, we realized that every single thing on it was going to cost money.

I have a little bit of money in the bank, but my parents won't let me touch that. It's supposed to help pay for my college education one day, where I will learn the skills I need to earn the money I'll need to pay back all the money I borrowed for the college education.

Isabella asked her mom for money, but since Isabella's mom has THREE children, and she is therefore three times meaner than a mom with only one, she said no. We tried to escape the room as soon as we saw her mouth begin to form ADULT WISDOM, but she's fast and hit us with, "You know, girls, the best things in life are free."

"Like money?" Isabella asked. "So, like, free money. Free money would be one of the best things in life, right?"

Isabella really excels at this sort of question, so her mom really excels at answering them.

"Go outside," she said.

Isabella stayed on the free money theme for a while. She said that her brothers have money, but explained that getting it for free could be a little inconvenient. According to Isabella, it could end up with me having to chew off a leg in order to free myself from whatever trap they had set. (That's right. "**Inconvenient**" is how she describes leg removal by chewing.)

I could see in her eyes that their money haunted her. If I were them, I would probably take a few precautions to protect it. Like that giant three-headed dog from *Harry Potter*.

Friday 06

Dear Dumb Diary,

Monday was the last day of school, but people who work at the school are there a few days longer than the kids.

I suspect they are there to finish our report cards, and to crate up the mean teachers and ship them to **Teacher Island** where they live for the summer, preying on one another in some kind of savage eat-or-be-eaten jungle environment.

Or, you know, just the report cards.

The reason I even brought this up was because yesterday was my Aunt Carol's last day at the school, and she stopped over for lunch when she was done. She asked how my vacation was going, because this is the sort of thing adults ask when they can't think of something interesting to say.

I told her about my **List of Summer Excellence** and how it was looking a little too spendy.

Aunt Carol told me that she and my mom used to do little jobs like babysit, rake leaves, or walk dogs for money. Then she said that my mom used to steal cars and sell them for money, too, but she only said that to upset my mom. (Aunt Carol may be secretly wearing a **WWMMSU** bracelet.)

Then my mom said Aunt Carol used to charge people five cents to clean out their trash cans with her face.

Then Aunt Carol said that right afterward, she would pay my mom a dollar to lick all the garbage flavor off her cheeks.

Even though this was all getting pretty ridiculous, I think they may have given me at least one pretty good idea: Never have a sister.

Saturday 07

Dear Dumb Diary,

I went five whole days without seeing or hearing from Angeline. I was beginning to get used to it. It's true that I have learned to overlook many of Angeline's flaws, like her **flawlessness,** but she can still be difficult to be around. Like when she's lit perfectly, for example.

To my extreme credit, I have learned to pretend to ignore Angeline's failure to not be perfect. So when Aunt Carol and Uncle Dan (the assistant principal at my school) brought Angeline over today, I didn't ask my attack dogs — Stinker and Stinkette — to bite her, or sit near her with their **epic ugliness** and **demonic fragrances**, or dribble their **putrid froth** on her, which might be worse than being bitten.

Angeline was all excited and told me and Isabella how much she had missed us this week. We made grunting sounds in response, which got Angeline all happy and chirpy because evidently we accidentally said, "Yeah! Us, too!" Maybe we did. I don't know, I don't speak **Blondese**.

Aunt Carol and Uncle Dan sat down and smiled and said they had something they wanted to share with us. Evidently, that often means "We're having a baby," because my mom exploded into this screaming volcano of laughter and hugged them and hugged me and hugged Stinker, which scared him and made him pee. And she started asking *when* and couldn't stop grinning.

At least that's what **"We have something to tell you"** means sometimes, but not this time. This time it meant that Aunt Carol and Uncle Dan were planning a trip to Screamotopia Amusement Park and wanted to know if Angeline, Isabella, and I wanted to go. This set off a secondary screaming volcano of laughter. We hugged them and hugged one another and hugged Stinker, which made him pee again. Then we started asking *when when when* and we couldn't stop grinning. If you do the math, you'll notice that New Baby to Mom = Amusement Park to Girl.

But since my Uncle Dan is an assistant principal — a **tricky creature** by nature — there was a catch. They explained it while we were spanking Stinker for peeing.

If we could raise the money for Screamotopia admission, Aunt Carol and Uncle Dan would drive us there and pick up the cost of the hotel so we could stay overnight. **I love hotels.** They're like magical apartments where you can dump a milk shake in the tub, and when you get back later, elves will have cleaned it all up.

My mom said okay, but she was a little mad that Aunt Carol hadn't talked to her **BEFORE** she told us. (When mom said "**BEFORE,**" she actually said it **IN ALL CAPITALS** like that. Moms can speak **IN ALL CAPITALS** when they want.)

Here's the hard part: We'll need a hundred dollars apiece, and we only have about three weeks to raise it.

Mom can speak in several FONTS as well.

Angeline's mom had already told Uncle Dan it was okay. We called Isabella's mom on speakerphone and she said it was okay, too. She joked that we should take Isabella's brothers and dad as well, and then there was a long silence.

It was one of those jokes where nobody laughs.

I know she would have brought them over THAT VERY MINUTE

Uncle Dan added the rule that we could not just ask family members to give or lend us the money. We agreed to the deal, and Uncle Dan made us shake on it with him. I never really realized how tiny my hand was until I saw it suffocated inside a big manly let's-make-a-deal handshake. I wonder if I could make money off business ladies who share this problem, by selling a line of business-lady oven mitts to help remedy **Tiny-Lady-Hand-Handshake Syndrome.**

We decided that the three of us will get together tomorrow and earn hundreds of dollars. I told them my intensely revolutionary idea to make money. I don't want to say too much right now, but it's a brand-new way to bring the intense and much-desired refreshments of indoors to an intensely outdoor and intensely convenient location where the customer will pay intensely for them. Isabella and Angeline agreed that the idea is so terrific and intense that we should start thinking about how we're going to spend all the **extra money** we'll make.

Sunday 08

Dear Dumb Diary,

Isabella slept over last night. This morning started with me asking my dad to drive us to the store to buy the stuff we needed to make money.

Dad immediately objected, partly because I woke up way too early again and it's a Sunday. But mostly because it required the spending of money and the moving of a butt on a Sunday morning. This is the day Dad traditionally sets aside to avoid moving his.

Other people's butts and money are not a problem for Dad, but he's pretty picky about HIS butt and HIS money and, in particular, separating one from the other.

Thankfully, Mom started writing a list of chores that needed to be done around the house. When Dad heard the sound of Mom's angry little pencil scratching out a list, he dragged us out to the car with a level of panic that I knew meant he would be willing to push it to the store if he had to.

We bought cups and powdered lemonade mix and a new plastic pitcher because our old one has a handle with chew marks on it. They were put there by me when I was a baby. It turns out that babies, with their fat legs, short arms, and desire to chew, are pretty much just miniature, blubbery **Tyrannosaurus rexes** on a never-ending hunt for wounded young triceratops — or plastic household items — to gnaw on.

See? pretty much the same animal.

By the time Angeline showed up, I had already made my **GRAND OPENING** sign for our lemonade stand. We'd finally decided to call it **IJA Lemonade**, a name created by using our first initials, which I don't think really reflected the entire scope of my vision for our establishment.

We stood out on my front lawn all afternoon, trying to get somebody to buy our lemonade. I'm confident that the cars that sped by at 40 miles per hour would have at least slowed down to consider making a beverage purchase at **Lemon-o-tastical-abulous Vegetarian Lemonade.** (That's what I wanted to call it, but Isabella wouldn't go for it on the grounds that it was stupid.) They might have even ordered something off the light lunch menu that I prepared.

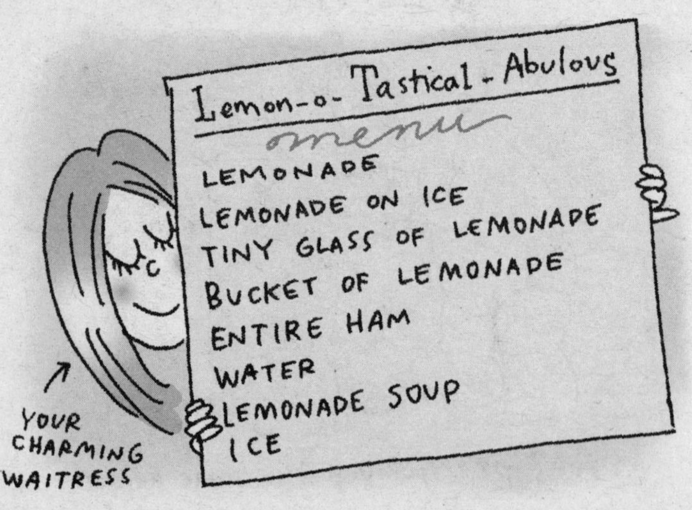

We were so desperate that I even ALMOST hoped that Mrs. Ryan across the street would bring over her crazy triplet sons. They're two years old, but they are as wild and screamy as baboons. (Mrs. Ryan always looks as though she just woke up from sleeping in a car trunk.)

Finally, after three full hours, we had our first customer. Cigarette Lady and her little grandson were out for a walk and he begged her to stop for a lemonade.

I don't know Cigarette Lady's real name, but she always smells like cigarettes. One time when my dad broke his leg, she brought down a cake she made that tasted like cigarettes. She has a little dog we call Smokey because every time he barks, he coughs and then spits something out.

"One, please," she said, and handed me a quarter that smelled like cigarettes.

Angeline picked up a cup and tilted the pitcher, then tilted it more and more. **Nothing came out.** Isabella grabbed the empty cup from her hand and gave it to Cigarette Grandson.

"Here you go," she said.

"But it's empty," he said.

"Yeah. It's the cup that costs a quarter," Isabella said. "The lemonade was free while supplies lasted, but the supply ran out."

I handed Cigarette Lady back her quarter. "Just kidding," I said. "I guess we sold out. Try back tomorrow."

Cigarette Grandson was crushed. I think when he stays there, his grandmother almost never takes him out, and the inside of her house has the aroma of an **active volcano.** We watched them walk back home. A few minutes after they went inside, we couldn't smell them anymore.

"What happened to all the lemonade?" I asked.

"Angeline drank it a little bit at a time when the two of us weren't looking," Isabella said quickly, adding, "I have to use your bathroom again."

Isabella ran inside, and Angeline and I started gathering up the lemonade stand stuff.

"I did not," Angeline said. She smiled pleasantly, which is exactly the kind of smile you want to push down somebody's throat at a moment when she probably single-handedly destroyed your lemonade stand/restaurant.

Dad told me not to worry about paying him back for the stuff we bought, but Mom reminded us that I had to, because that was the deal I made. Hey, way to go, Mom, with that memory thing, for the first time in history when Dad's not being a cheapskate.

Monday 09

Dear Dumb Diary,

I truly believe I could solve everybody's problems if they would do just one simple thing: **Everything I say.**

Today on the phone, Angeline and I went over our follow-up plan for the lemonade stand. Isabella couldn't come over because she drank too much of something yesterday — but it wasn't lemonade — and she still felt a little sick.

I told Angeline about these books I read where the girls were babysitters and I think they also solved crimes. I thought it would be a great idea if we raised money by babysitting and/or solving crimes.

Here were my points:

1) Who doesn't love little kids? **Parents**, that's who. And that's why babysitters are always in demand.
2) It is probably not that hard because all of the babysitters in the books have plenty of extra time to solve crimes and have crushes and be rock stars.
3) Angeline cannot drink a child, so she won't screw up our business.

Angeline objected to the child-drinking reference because it's important to her to continue to deny that she stole our lemonade. Whatever. **I'm past that.**

I tossed out a name for our babysitting service, which I think is brilliant: **Baby-o-tastical-abulous.** Angeline didn't really respond to it one way or another (envy can make a person speechless), but she said that babysitting isn't always as easy as you think. Then I asked her how she knew, and my penetrating line of crime-solving-babysitter questioning forced her to confess something:

She **DOES** babysit sometimes.

I know, right? Behind our backs, while we're trying to maintain the Baby-o-tastical-abulous babysitting service and children's boutique, she's competing with us!

I know she felt guilty about it because she said she'd ask her mom's friend if she needs a babysitter this week. If she does, the three of us can babysit her client together at Angeline's house.

I called Isabella with the news. She was really excited about the whole idea except for the babysitting part. Babies don't really like Isabella for some reason, and I don't know why. My theory is that it's the smell of the soap she uses, or the reflections on her glasses, or maybe they're just not very tolerant of people who yell at babies.

Anyway, Isabella finally agreed and even came up with a great idea of taking pictures of us to use in flyers to advertise Baby-o-tastical-abulous, which is the name of our company even though Angeline and Isabella believe it is not.

some babies are against yelling

I was so excited when Angeline called.

Now **THAT'S** a sentence I never thought I would be capable of writing. Unless it went on to say: ***. . . out helplessly from the bottom of an elevator shaft.***

Tomorrow morning we actually get to babysit at her house! Her mom's friend is going to leave her one-year-old in our official care for about three hours. I have to get to sleep now so that we can begin our exciting new career tomorrow.

But before I do, maybe I'll just sketch out a few of the baby fashions I expect we'll soon be offering in our boutique.

Tuesday 10

Dear Dumb Diary,

Okay, Dumb Diary, before I tell you about today, I need to make one point very clear: As always, **nothing is my fault.**

We showed up at Angeline's house just before eleven and met Angeline's mom's friend, Mrs. Twining, and her little boy, Ricky. Ricky is the very fat one-year-old individual that we were contracted to babysit.

Angeline has babysat Fat Ricky several times before, and could have easily handled the whole thing while Isabella and I watched TV. But that didn't really seem to be in the spirit of what we wanted to do when we launched Baby-o-tastical-abulous Vegetarian Day Care and Boutique. I mean: We all needed to play a part.

Babies, like people, need to be fed, and given beverages, and according to Angeline, they want to **play**. So Isabella and I sat down on the floor and played with Ricky while she got his lunch ready.

We weren't quite sure how to do it, so Isabella poked him a few times to see if he liked that. He didn't. I let him play with my shoe, and he was perfectly happy until Angeline came in and pulled it out of his mouth. That makes me doubt if she really knows what makes children happy. Our organization should review her credentials.

Perhaps out of anger at Angeline for taking his favorite shoe-toy away from him, Ricky stinkfully performed a dirty diaper.

I have spent a lot of time around **BFO (Beagle Fart Odor)**, so Ricky's smell did not instantly murder me, although an extended period of time in his odor cloud would have massacred us all. I wondered if it was possible for Ricky to have somehow eaten several dozen beagle farts, but I'm not sure that's even possible.

Angeline held her nose and said she'd take care of it, but luckily for her, Isabella was there to help out. Isabella is very difficult to disgust due to the fact that her mean older brothers have subjected her to a **lifetime of grossness**.

"I know what to do," she said, and took Ricky into the other room. "C'mon, Ricky. Let's put a fresh diaper on you."

Angeline looked a little concerned, but I pointed out that Isabella actually had little cousins of her own and knew how a diaper was operated.

After that, we gave Ricky lunch, which was pretty funny because when Isabella put her sunglasses on him, he looked a lot like her grandpa and how he eats.

We all started laughing really hard and that made Ricky laugh, too. So hard, in fact, that he started to stink again, also like Isabella's grandpa. (Nobody in her family is allowed to tell him jokes.)

So Isabella just picked up Ricky and whisked him away. "Let's put a fresh diaper on you," she said. Angeline and I were surprised that she wasn't really very angry about it.

For the next two hours, we were actually a pretty good team. Angeline would tell me how to play with Ricky, I would do the actual non-shoe playing, and whenever Ricky started smelling icky, Isabella would take him into the next room and put a fresh diaper on him.

I never knew that babies needed so many diapers. Angeline said it was pretty unusual for Ricky to go through seven diapers in three hours, but maybe he had a big breakfast or something.

Anyway, Baby-o-tastical-abulous looked like a huge success, based on projections I did using the math that teachers always said I would need in the Real World. Mrs. Twining was sure to tell her friends how great we were, and I figured we would have a whole ranch full of babies to sit before you knew it.

Hello, Screamotopia!

When Angeline's mom and Mrs. Twining finally got back to Angeline's, everybody was really happy because we were going to get paid and Ricky was still in one piece and we were **going to get paid**.

Ricky started bouncing around and began to stink again. Isabella said, "No worries. I'll put a fresh diaper on him before we go."

Mrs. Twining laughed and said, "Oh, don't be silly. Your job is done, girls. I'll change his diaper." She picked him up and walked into the other room,

After about a minute, she called Angeline's mom to come in.

Then they walked little Ricky out. All he had on were his diapers.

All eight of them.

He was wearing the one he wore over to Angeline's, plus the **seven** that Isabella had layered on. We didn't notice because, as I mentioned earlier, Ricky is on the tubby side of fat.

Aaaaaand we're not getting the endorsement from Mrs. Twining I'd hoped for.

Isabella said she knew that she was supposed to change Ricky's diapers, but it occurred to her that if she just covered the dirty one with a fresh one it would lock in the stink, and wasn't that the point anyway? (When you think about it, she was pretty much right.)

When the stink started leaking out, Isabella got the impression that Ricky was kind of messing with her, so she kept adding layers. She asked Mrs. Twining if she ever got that impression about Ricky, or if Ricky maybe had a **bad attitude** or something.

It got a little worse from there, and we got a lecture from Mrs. Twining about how important it is to take care of babies properly, and Isabella got a little angry and said it wasn't our fault that her kid poops his pants.

In the end, we **did** get paid, which was a relief because at one point somebody said something about somebody's baby looking like an ape. See, this is all about timing: You should always wait to tell the mom her baby looks like an ape until *AFTER* you get paid, because the ape observation (though accurate) probably cost us our tip. Still, we pulled in twenty dollars, which means that when we subtract what I owed my dad we have, like, ten dollars now. That's PURE PROFIT.

But I don't think we're going to babysit in this town again. So now that Baby-o-tastical-abulous is officially closed, we need a new line of work. Ten dollars won't buy you much amusement at an amusement park.

Wednesday 11

Dear Dumb Diary,

Isabella was in no mood to work on our amusement park goal today. She said she had determined that there would be a brief period of time where her brothers would be out of the house and her mom would be in the yard, and she planned to use that twelve and a half minutes to go online.

It's not like she's **NEVER** allowed to go online, in spite of an attempt when she was four to **break the Internet** out of revenge, after her mean older brothers showed her a video that scared the cupcakes out of her.

The good news is that you can't break the Internet, no matter how many feet of cable you manage to drag out of the wall.

The bad news (according to Isabella) is that you can't break the Internet, no matter how many feet of cable you manage to drag out of the wall.

She says that she just prefers to go online privately, when there's nobody around to interrupt her with little distractions like being grounded for going online.

Angeline called to say she was going to be babysitting Icky Ricky again today, but Mrs. Twining specifically said that she wanted **ONLY** Angeline on the job. I believe that Angeline was telling the truth about Mrs. Twining, because Angeline probably blamed the multi-diapering on Isabella instead of accepting some of the blame herself for **NOT** telling Isabella that Mrs. Twining had some sort of weird thing against diaper layering.

I'm not sure how I feel about Angeline taking advantage of the good name of Baby-o-tastical-abulous behind our backs (even though she did it in front of our faces and isn't using the name), and I told her so.

She said she'd be willing to put her earnings from babysitting into the mutual **AMUSEMENT PARK FUND**, but that she was doing this one for free to make it up to Mrs. Twining for the multi-diapering incident.

That seemed fair to me. When I called Isabella it seemed fair to her, too, after forty minutes of arguing.

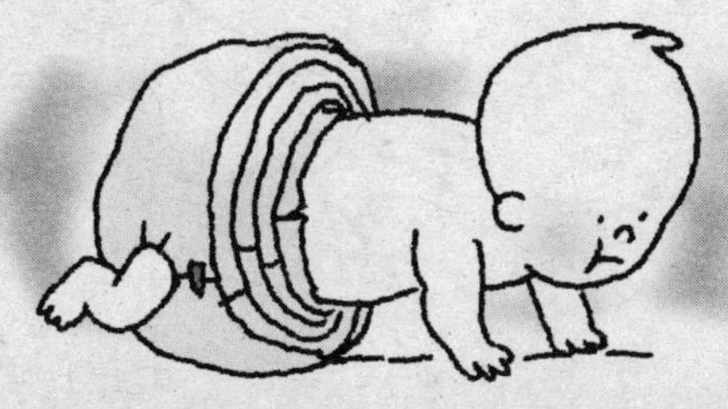

face it, lady.
this is a
great idea.

I ran a new moneymaking plan past my mom this morning, but here's something I've noticed about my mom: She **SAYS** that she likes the idea of me making my own money, but when it's time for her to prove it — like when I told her I'd clean my room for twenty dollars — she doesn't come through.

And here's the thing: She's seen my room. She **KNOWS** that twenty dollars is a bargain. She even got angry when I told her that I could offer her a light room cleaning at five dollars off my regular low low price.

When Dad got home, I ran some new moneymaking ideas past him. He said he'd think about them, which is **Dad Language** for "I will not be thinking about these."

He also said something about just giving me the money, but Mom walked in and he got real quiet.

A few new moneymaking ideas

when somebody farts, I charge them to take the blame.

I eat the rejected things from the plates of people who don't own dogs.

I lure all known clowns into an enormous trap and then charge the world an appropriate gigantic fee.

Thursday 12

Dear Dumb Diary,

This morning, my mom said that she'd pay us to wash her car today. That gave me a **terrific idea**: What if I just waited until it rained and then charged her for that? That's really about the same thing, right?

She said it wasn't the same, so I got another **terrific idea.**

"What if Angeline and Isabella and I washed cars in the driveway today?" I said. I suggested we charge fifty dollars per car.

Mom said that people can get their cars washed at the regular old car wash for five bucks. So MAYBE they'd be willing to spend $4.50 on ours, you know, just because adults love to help kids.

I'm not sure how chiseling us out of fifty cents qualifies as love, but whatever. We'll take it.

We waited until after lunch to get started, because we wanted it to be nice and warm out. Angeline and Isabella both brought sponges and rags over and we had a couple buckets of soapy water. I made a sign by cutting big numbers out of red construction paper and gluing them to a poster board. I wanted to put the name of our car wash on it, but Isabella said it was dumb so I don't even want to tell you what it was. (But I'll give you a hint: It was a **fantastical-abulous** and **vegetarian** name.)

Our plan was that Isabella would hold up the sign, Angeline would direct cars up the driveway, and then the three of us would wash each car. I would collect the money while Angeline and Isabella went back and got into position for the next car.

All those cars. **All that money**, right?

Wrong. Not only is my neighborhood not into lemonade, they really aren't into automotive hygiene, either.

Every time a car would go by, Isabella would shake the sign like crazy, and we'd all yell and they'd pretend not to see us, and Cigarette Lady would come out and ask us what all the yelling was about.

We'd tell her we were having a car wash and she'd yell back, "A GAH BAH? WHAT'S A GAH BAH?" Then we'd yell back, "A CAR WASH!"

And then she'd yell, "OKAY, THEN I'LL FNURGHLMKMGH." That *Fnurghlmkmgh* sound at the end is the nasty coughing noise she makes because when heavy smokers shout, sometimes their lungs try to climb out of their throats.

Then she would go back inside until the next car drove by, and we'd start all over again.

It had been a long day. We were all in a pretty lousy mood and were just getting ready to quit when we saw Cigarette Lady walk Cigarette Grandson out to her giant car. She slowly and carefully backed it out of her garage, and slowly and carefully rolled down her driveway, and slowly and carefully took out one of her own bushes.

Then she slowly and carefully drove over to my driveway, where she slowly and carefully almost ran over Isabella as she pulled in.

For some reason, the older people get, the bigger the cars they drive. This is totally backward, because the older they get, the worse they drive, and so they are getting more and more dangerous to the rest of us as their cars get bigger and bigger. As you get older, you should have to drive *smaller and smaller* cars. By the time you're as old as Cigarette Lady, you should be on a unicycle.

Cigarette Lady said she wanted a car wash. Like I mentioned, she has a giant car, so it took a lot longer to wash than I thought it would. It wasn't very dirty, because she only uses it to drive to the store to buy cigarettes and to run over her bushes. She probably buys medicine, too, because old people are really fond of medicine, and maybe like one bag of groceries a year, because old ladies hardly eat anything. I'm not kidding: I remember one time when my grandma saved the other half of a peanut for later.

When we were all done, she pulled out her giant purse and started digging around in it. After pulling out a pack of cigarettes, a lighter, a pack of gum, a rain bonnet, a handkerchief, a pack of cigarettes, some matches, nasal spray, and a pack of cigarettes, she finally found her little-old-lady wallet.

She unsnapped the pocket, smiled, and handed me one dollar.

One dollar.

I stood there with my hand out, waiting for the rest of the money, and she stood there, smiling back at me. I raised my eyebrows a little, to indicate that I was expecting something, and she raised hers back at me.

I raised mine higher and she raised hers as well. I raised mine again, and so did she. I kept raising them until I finally ran out of forehead. (Turns out Cigarette Lady has a pretty plentiful forehead area.) I didn't want to be pushy, but I couldn't hold back any longer.

"It's not a dollar," I said cheerfully. "The car wash. We're not charging a dollar."

"I know, sweetie." She coughed, and as she did, I noticed the Ryan triplets looking out their front window, screaming and pointing at something on their lawn. It was red. It was paper. **It was the number "4."**

"Urp," I said, nicely summing up exactly what I was feeling.

Cigarette Lady was waiting for her *change*.

She put out her hand and I gave her fifty cents. What else could I do? Then she slowly and carefully backed out of my driveway, drove slowly and carefully over to her house, and slowly and carefully took out one of her bushes again.

I picked up the poster board Isabella had been waving so furiously.

"You shook the sign too hard. You shook the four right off it. It doesn't say $4.50 anymore. It says fifty cents," I said. "Cigarette Lady only paid us fifty cents because that's what our sign says now."

"You didn't use enough glue," Isabella said. "So you owe Angeline and me $4.00, plus a tip," she said.

"Let's try again tomorrow," Angeline said, and she was using that calm, optimistic voice people use just before you tell them to shut up.

"Shut up, Angeline," Isabella and I said in perfect unison as if we had practiced it **a million times,** when in reality we only practiced it, like, a dozen times.

"You should have noticed that the number blew off," Isabella said to her.

"Isabella's right," I added, knowing that Isabella wasn't right. It's funny how much easier it is to tell that something isn't right when it comes out of somebody else's mouth.

We cleaned up the stuff silently and grunted our good-byes at one another.

When you calculate what we spent for the soap, and add the microscopic payment we got from Cigarette Lady, our AMUSEMENT PARK FUND is now worth exactly $5.50.

I'm going to bed.

Baby Jamie: $ 0.00

current Jamie: $ 5.50

40-YEAR-OLD JAMIE: $ 100.00

At this rate, I won't be able to buy a car until I'm 1000.

FRIDAY 13

Dear Dumb Diary,

Isabella is really into this moneymaking thing now. The failed car wash really got her going. This morning, she came over first thing and took my picture, because she says we need to make flyers to advertise our different services. She mussed up my hair a little, because that will let people know that we work hard. I asked her why I had to wear a black T-shirt for the picture, and she said it would make me look like a **ninja** or a **seal**, which both also work hard.

I never had the impression that seals work hard, and I questioned that but Isabella said maybe seals wouldn't, but ***Ninja Seals*** would. And she said it with this slow, smiling nod that made me think that she must be right. Isabella is pretty good at convincing people of things.

I offered to help with the flyers, being great at that sort of thing with all of my **Art Skills**, but Isabella said she wanted to do this one by herself. It's nice to give people space when they want to try new things, especially when they say so with a threatening undertone.

Always take the Hint.

Isabella wanted to use our computer while she was over, but her mom called my mom months ago and told her **NOT** to let Isabella use our computer. Ever.

Mom just added that to a long list of instructions that Isabella's mom has given her regarding Isabella.

Since Isabella couldn't use the computer, we went over to Angeline's to take her picture. When we got there, Emmily was there. This surprised me because I suddenly remembered that we had decided she was our friend, but in the two weeks that we'd been out of school, I had forgotten that she existed.

Emmily is very nice, but not exactly bright. Let's just say her koala can't quite make it to the top of the eucalyptus tree. One time she was supposed to bring ice to the end-of-year party at school, and she actually asked us if we could **write down the recipe.**

Angeline didn't want Isabella to take the picture today, because she was afraid that Emmily would think that she had been left out. Isabella said that Emmily wouldn't think she was left out because Emmily doesn't do a lot of thinking. To prove it, she asked her a question.

"Emmily, can you think of a good way for us to make money?" Isabella asked her.

"Yes," Emmily said.

She stood there, looking at us.

"Okay. What would it be?" Isabella asked her very slowly.

"Oh," she said as if somebody had just jabbed her in the ribs. "You could earn it somehow."

Just as Isabella was about to explode, Emmily added, "And I could help you."

Oh. My. Gosh. Our exciting new vegetarian company was getting its first employee! For a moment, I wished I liked coffee so I could ask Emmily to go make me some.

Angeline put her hand on Emmily's shoulder. "We're saving up to go to Screamotopia. And you won't be able to go with us. You would be helping us raise money for something you won't get to do," Angeline said, doing her best to gently blow the deal.

"That's okay," Emmily said, and she meant it, too. Emmily is that special sort of generous person that people are **before they know any better.**

"Mostly, you'll be helping me," Isabella said, and Emmily grinned. "You'll be, like, my secretary or my assistant. I'll have you working on very special projects — ones I couldn't trust to the other employees."

I felt a chill go down my back. Emmily was smiling and nodding. Isabella could have thrown a saddle on Emmily and ridden her around if she wanted to. I'll bet that if Isabella was a bad person, she could really take advantage of her friends. **Good thing she's so nice.**

"Emmily, do you have a computer at home? One where I could go online?" Isabella asked.

"Sure, and it has one of those —"

Isabella cut her off in mid-sentence and began to run toward Emmily's house, which was just four houses away from Angeline's. Emmily did her best to keep up.

"Bye, guys! See you later," Isabella yelled.

We didn't see her later.

Once they left, Angeline started to brush her hair. Did she have the brush in her pocket? In her ear? From nowhere, a brush just appeared. How do people with beautiful hair do that?

She started looking a little sad, which you don't normally see on Angeline, no matter how much you hope for it.

"Do you think we're going to make the money?" she asked. I didn't really have an answer.

By the time I got home, I didn't have any appetite at all, so I practiced some vegetarianism against the dinner my mom made . . . including the vegetables in it.

Right now all I can think about is the amazing stuff they probably have at Screamotopia, and how I hope hope hope we get to go.

Merry-go-rounds with real animals.
All the games have huge CASH PRIZES. And diamonds. And RUBIES.
High-Quality cotton candy that's more like ANGORA CANDY.
If somebody's hair is too pretty, they have to wear a special bonnet.

Saturday 14

Dear Dumb Diary,

I had to do regular old nonpaying work today. Mom wanted me to clean my room. Mom and I have the exact same conversation every time she asks me to clean my room, and it just does not seem to sink in.

"Mom, if I've told you once, I've told you a thousand times: Eeeeeyaaagh."

Dumb Diary, I know you don't have ears, but this is a sort of combination grunt/groan sound I make that increases in volume as I walk up the stairs to my room. It conveys an entire spectrum of feelings, as well as a detailed argument against cleaning my room, but my mother never seems to understand it. Usually, it just makes her angrier and occasionally swearier, and I wind up having to clean up my room anyway.

And, if you can believe it, I have to do it for free.

I'm against cleaning my room, because I feel it promotes housework in general, but today I think it also promoted a type of **archaeology** – and archaeology can lead to **treasure**.

I uncovered several very interesting artifacts today. Here is the list of things I found that I managed to rescue before Stinker and his dogdaughter Stinkette could chew them to bits:

- Handful of old doll clothes
- Souvenir thing my grandma gave me from someplace she went in China or Cleveland or somewhere
- Old fairy-tale book purchased at garage sale for fifty cents
- Half sandwich probably once owned by caveman
- Evidence of an ancient carpet buried below the deepest level, possibly put there by dinosaurs

I thought about having a garage sale where we could sell our old stuff to make money, but I've had bad experiences with garage sales. I don't like people exploring and judging my nasty old stuff while I'm standing there.

It's like "Yes, sir, I *know* that sale item is **super, super, super gross**. That's why it's ***for sale***. I'm keeping all my good stuff, Einstein."

That's when it occurred to me. We could sell our old nasty stuff online . . . on eBay. That way, we wouldn't have to look directly into the eyes of the people we were offending with our rubbish. I was so excited that I called Isabella. Tomorrow we'll see if we can get our moms together on this to let us do it.

If this works, it will probably be the beginning of our own personal auction website — do I really have to tell you the name? It's www.tastical.auction.abulous.unicorn. It will probably be revolutionary.

Sunday 15

Dear Dumb Diary,

Isabella was at my house before any of us woke up this morning, and she totally scared my dad when he opened the door to get the newspaper. Isabella was just snoozing on our porch, but she can't help it if all of her sleeping positions look like the positions that police find the victim in when they arrive at a crime scene.

Dad let Isabella into my room to wake me up. I have no idea how long she was there before I opened my eyes, but when I did, I saw her quietly going through my drawers, probably organizing my socks and stuff. **So helpful.**

When Mom finally got up, she and Isabella's mom talked on the phone about setting up an account on eBay so we could sell our junk. Remember that Isabella's mom had said that Isabella should not be allowed on our computer, so they had to talk for a long time, and Mom closed the door so we couldn't hear. Later on, I learned from my mom that Isabella's mom had a rather long list of warnings to give her, and instructed her to be very careful about how she selected the password on the account because Isabella can be very **playful** about trying to crack passwords.

"**Playful**" is the word my mom used. I've never heard anybody else describe Isabella in that exact way. I wonder how Mom would describe other people?

Isabella photographed my old doll clothes and the fairy-tale book to sell. My mom wouldn't let me sell the souvenir thing my grandma got me, and Stinker ate the prehistoric sandwich.

My mom set up the account, and then Isabella started telling her exactly what to do to post the information, upload the pictures, all that stuff.

Pretty soon Isabella was working the keyboard and my mom was just watching her. Isabella was very fast at picking up exactly how to manage the account, even though she had never done it before. What can I say? My BFF's a genius.

We called Angeline and asked if she had anything to sell, and she said yes. Plus, Isabella still needed to photograph her for the flyers she wants to make. So after lunch, my mom drove us over to Angeline's house. I remember it all very clearly, because people say you always remember your first genuine heart failure.

Friday, when I saw Angeline last, she was as I've always known her: A disturbingly pretty girl with annoyingly beautiful long blond hair, and some other qualities I can't really recall.

Today when we went over, she was different. Way different. **Totally totally totally totally totally totally totally totally totally totally totally different.**

It was as though Angeline was no longer Angeline. She looked more like the framework on which they were constructing an Angeline, but hadn't quite finished. And that's because . . .

Angeline cut off her hair. **All of it.**

Well, not all of it. She still has eyebrows and eyelashes and a little bit of hair on her head, and if people like Angeline had nose hairs or arm hairs she'd still have those, but the long cascading waterfall of golden shimmering silk is **GONE**.

Isabella and I just stood there for a second not knowing what to say, until Isabella quietly said a swear and then another one. Generally, I'm not for swears because they usually indicate an underdeveloped vocabulary, but if Isabella hadn't done it, I might have, although I would have selected one less nasty.

I remember one time I saw this machine on TV that they roll across fields to harvest stalks of corn. I always thought it would be nice if they would roll it over Angeline and **harvest her hair**.

Without her hair, I knew that Angeline wouldn't be that pretty anymore. I had tested the theory on Barbies, and it was always the same result: Without her hair, Barbie resembled a toe with a face. I knew that Angeline would also look like a toe, and the world would be happier.

Except I was wrong. With less hair, our eyes were drawn to the rest of Angeline's face — which, it turned out, was **far prettier** than we'd ever noticed before. This seemed to make Isabella angrier than I could have expected, and she started to yell at Angeline.

"Why did you get your hair cut off???" she demanded.

"Just because," Angeline said.

"You didn't ask us what we thought," Isabella shot back.

Angeline's jaw pushed forward and her eyebrows flattened. "**It's my hair**, Isabella. I can do anything I want with it."

"No. No. That's where you're mistaken, Rapunzel," Isabella said angrily. "When there are other people involved, you can't just go and do something like that."

I had no idea this whole thing would make Isabella so upset. I mean, c'mon Isabella, it's just hair. Shimmering, sparkling, radiant, heavenly, magnificent hair. **No big deal.**

"Besides, Isabella," Angeline said, "you wear *your* hair kind of short. Why is it only a good idea for you?"

And that was how it ended. Isabella stormed off to Emmily's house, and Angeline was in no mood to talk **or** raise money. So I went home and walked Stinker and Stinkette, just to see if we might enjoy starting a dog-walking service to raise money that we'd call **the Dog-o-tastical-abulous Walking and Grooming Emporium.**

It seemed like a good idea until they both went to the bathroom for the third time. Then I realized that walking more dogs would mean picking up more **yuckies.**

I think I'm closing this business before I open it, like I have with several others.

Monday 16

Dear Dumb Diary,

Emmily called this morning to pass along a memo from her boss, Isabella, that we should get together later to discuss the personal style our company is projecting.

I made Emmily put Isabella on the phone and reminded her that Emmily was not just her personal employee, but that I owned her, too.

I could hear Isabella immediately turn to Emmily and say, "Jamie owns you, too."

"Okay," Emmily said.

I know that *technically* I can't really exactly own a person, and that *technically*, Emmily is a person. But explaining things like this to Emmily makes her eyes involuntarily cross and stay crossed for hours, so we're just better off using the term "own."

Isabella got back on the phone and said that she had been thinking about Angeline's haircut. She decided that it gave our operation a more professional look. It said to the world: *Look, if you need a job done, we can do it, and we won't waste valuable seconds putting our hair back in a ponytail before we do.*

And then she set down the phone and cut off Emmily's hair.

I heard it all. I heard her tell Emmily to sit down, I heard the scissors snipping, I heard Emmily ask what was going on, and I heard Isabella say to shut up and stop squirming.

When Isabella picked up the phone she was panting a little.

"See? You're next. We're on our way over," she huffed.

In the movies, the crazy psychopaths don't usually call you up and tell you that they're on their way over and they're bringing an employee to help hold you down, right? **Here's why:** It would give you time to go tell your mom on them. Plus, employees usually seek more secure types of employment than with crazies.

By the time Isabella and Emmily arrived, Mom was waiting at the door for them.

"No haircuts," she said to Isabella. And then she turned to say something to Emmily, but Emmily's recent haircut made Mom say the same swear that Isabella had said yesterday.

"I'm going to even it up," Isabella explained, gesturing to Emmily's hair. My mom gently offered to help with that, even though I'm sure I heard her do that swear again under her breath.

While my mom called Emmily's mom (to explain things and get permission to do **first aid** on her hair), Isabella and I talked it out in the living room.

"Jamie," she said, "we all have short hair now. It's kind of our look. I'm not pressuring you, and you don't have to get yours cut if you don't want to. But if you don't want to, promise me you'll close your eyes and ask yourself this simple question out loud: *Why am I such a stupid buttface loser who won't say okay?*"

And while I was asking myself that question with my eyes closed, Isabella quickly cut a **huge patch of hair** off the left side of my head.

"Why. Did. You. Do. That?" I asked, stunned.

"You said *okay*," Isabella said. "Now let me finish."

"I only said *okay* because it's the last word in the question you asked me to consider."

Isabella shrugged. "Oh. I probably shouldn't have phrased it that way," she said. "You were confused by it. But you **did** say *okay*."

She had a point.

I took the handful of hair and showed it to my mom. I explained what happened, and how it was a misunderstanding, and how misunderstandings can cause a person to innocently lunge at you with scissors.

Mom was less upset than I thought she'd be. She said it would grow back, and that maybe I'd like short hair for the summertime anyway.

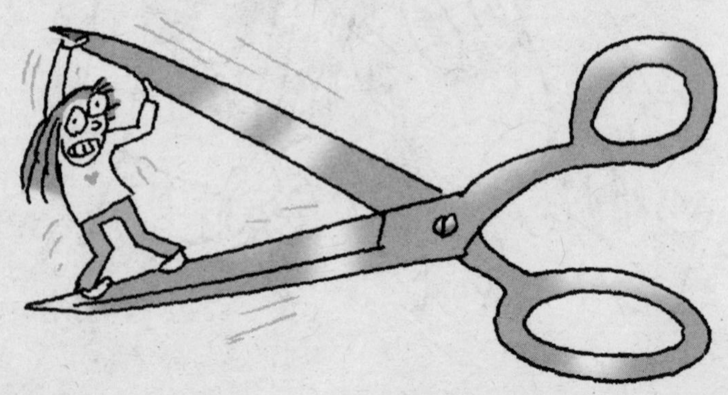

I had to think for a moment. There were ramifications.

In the end, I sat down, and Mom cut the rest of it.

Angeline came over later so the four of us could compare our short hair, and I was really surprised at how **adorable** we all looked. Isabella and Angeline made up from their little issue yesterday, although neither one of them apologized. (It was one of those invisible apologies people do when they don't want to fight anymore but they don't want to actually say "I'm sorry," either, so both parties silently agree to pretend it never happened.)

Isabella took pictures of Angeline and Emmily, but only Angeline had to wear the black T-shirt like I had. That's because Emmily is not going in our ads. I wrote that last sentence in a whisper.

Angeline also brought over a few items for our eBay auction, which included a plush bear, an unopened bottle of old lady perfume her aunt gave her, and an ugly vase. These are, of course, **horrible junk**, and therefore will fit in perfectly with my items. We're going to stack so much cheese! ("Stack cheese" is cool-talk for "make money." At least I think it's still cool.)

Isabella still hasn't chosen her items, she says, but she's taking care of posting all of our stuff in the meantime.

We didn't really talk money today, and Angeline hardly even bothered me — even though she insisted on helping my mom clean up the haircut mess like a big kiss-up. I think she mostly didn't bother me because she didn't have her hair anymore, just like the rest of us.

I wonder if this is why old guys and tiny babies get along so well with each other. Mutual baldness takes the pressure off.

Tuesday 17

Dear Dumb Diary,

I had planned to sleep in today. Instead, I woke up screaming because it suddenly occurred to me that, if my calculations are correct, we've passed the halfway point toward earning money for Screamotopia . . . and we have **five dollars and fifty cents**. That means, if my calculations are correct, by the end of the month we will have about eleven dollars, which means, if my calculations are correct, we are going to crash and burn. This also clearly demonstrates why I have always been against calculations.

Isabella came over early and suggested that I go start a dog-walking business while she checked to see how we were doing on eBay.

I told her that I had considered it, but didn't want to do that business because of the **double extra-intensity** of the grossness involved with cleaning up after additional poop machines.

Isabella had predicted this, and said that she had Emmily waiting outside to do all of the dog walking for me.

"I already told her everything she has to do. Just go outside and . . . you know, **'activate'** her," Isabella said.

And there Emmily was, standing on my porch, awaiting activation.

"You really want to walk dogs for us?" I asked her.

"Okay," she answered with her typical stupid sweetness, and I felt a wrenching, stabbing pain of guilt for taking advantage of her that way. **Then it passed and I was fine.**

But I had no idea what to charge our customers. "Just ask for fifty cents, I guess, or a dollar. And just walk the dogs up and down the street here. And don't go up to anybody's door you don't know," I said.

Emmily stepped off my porch, but to me, it seemed like I was sending her **off a cliff**.

"Wait!" I cried. "Don't do that. **ONLY** go over to Cigarette Lady's house. See if she wants you to walk Smokey. Did Isabella tell you that you have to clean up after the dog?"

Emmily's eyes got wider than usual. "She said to just kick it into the bushes. Or stomp it into the grass so nobody can see it."

You have to hand it to Isabella: They *are* pretty good ideas, especially considering that those aren't our shoes that Emmily's wearing.

And off our employee went. I watched her cross the street and walk up to Cigarette Lady's door, then I headed back inside to see how high the bidding had gotten on our auction items.

"It's going to take a week," Isabella said. "So stop asking me every day."

I asked how she got into the account without my mom signing her in, and she said my mom made it very clear to her that she was okay with Isabella managing the account by selecting a password that was so obvious for Isabella to guess.

I reminded her that time was slipping away and we were still **way off** the total we needed and that if we didn't start planning, we were really going to have a problem. Then Isabella and I were horrified because for a moment, it seemed as though **my mom's voice** had just popped out of my mouth.

Pretty soon, we were both trying to say things our parents would say.

"Jamie," I said like my dad, "stop sitting on Stinker while I'm trying to watch baseball and football and eat and shave."

"Isabella," Isabella said in a low voice like her dad's, "finish your milk and who broke this?"

"Don't stand there with the refrigerator door open, young lady!" I mommed.

"Why are there all these **human teeth** on the dinner table?" Isabella scolded.

I was getting ready to ask Isabella about that last one when we noticed Emmily across the street, walking Cigarette Grandson on a leash.

We went out to talk to her. It turns out that Cigarette Grandson's name is Joey. Maybe that sounds enough like Smokey that Cigarette Lady thought Emmily was asking to take **him** for a walk.

"She understands that she has to pay, right?" Isabella asked, grabbing briefly at Joey's leash as if she might toss him up in a tree if the answer was **no.**

Emmily pulled a dollar out of her pocket and showed it to us. "She paid in advance."

We shrugged and agreed that it was okay. Joey had lost all of his dignity of course, but dignity almost never shows up on a list of things three-year-olds treasure most.

Wednesday 18

Dear Dumb Diary,

Angeline and I met over at Isabella's house this afternoon. We called Emmily, but there was no answer.

Isabella's mom is a great cook, so her house always smells incredible. Once, when I was little, I secretly tasted their couch because I thought maybe their entire house was made out of lasagna. It wasn't. It just tasted couchy. Maybe a little bit chairy.

Today, I asked her mom for ideas on how we could make money for Screamotopia.

She thought for a minute, and said she'd give us the full three hundred dollars if we'd go upstairs and clean Isabella's brothers' room. Isabella immediately said no, but Angeline and I thought it sounded like easy money. I've cleaned my room before. I couldn't imagine that anybody's room could be any **worse.**

Isabella's mom handed me a garbage bag and gave Angeline a snow shovel. Then she and Isabella took us upstairs, down the hall, and stopped ten feet from the door. Even Isabella's dog, Bubs, stopped.

"It's right there," her mom said. "First door on the left."

"Is anybody in there?" I asked.

"I don't think so," Isabella said. "I think I heard them leave this morning. Knock first, just to make sure."

I knocked and knocked. **No answer.** Angeline knocked. No answer. So I opened the door and looked inside.

And here's the thing about iPods: iPods are **LOUD**. Really loud. So loud, in fact, that sometimes you can't hear somebody knocking on your bedroom door. And if your bedroom is **gross**, and you're **gross**, and you happen to be engaged in one of your main **gross** hobbies (seriously, who would even guess you *could* bite your own toenails?), you really don't expect to look up and see two girls standing there doing their best not to barf into your **gross** room, which, by the way, would **NOT** be any grosser as a result.

After an hour-long shower, I finally called Isabella and asked her to apologize to her mom for knocking her down in the hallway on my run down the stairs and out the door and all the way to my house.

She said Angeline was right behind me. I said that I remembered her screaming, but it turned out that was actually Isabella's brother, who had been hit by a flying snow shovel.

Of course, everyone understood that we were passing on her mom's offer to clean her brothers' room. Isabella and I talked about making Emmily do it, but we felt that it would be a little too much to expect of her, **based on just the underpants alone.**

I could try to piece together what I remember of the room, although my damaged psychology would surely prevent me from recalling any particularly horrifying details. Your brain does this, you know, to protect your sanity.

Oh, **P.S.** Isabella is coming over later tonight to work on our eBay thing.

Thursday 19

Dear Dumb Diary,

I was at Angeline's most of the day today. Isabella and I went over to try a combination lemonade stand/car wash, which we called **Lemon-o-tastical Carwash-o-tabulous**, except Angeline and Isabella wouldn't call it that because they said it was stupid.

We thought that things might be different over by Angeline's house, and we were right.

It was worse.

We didn't sell even **one glass** of lemonade. Some little kids stopped and stood there staring at us and said they didn't have any money, so bighearted Isabella generously offered to give them a glass for free if one of them would eat an ant. I didn't even feel bad about that, because at first they thought I was a boy.

And nobody on the whole street wanted his or her car washed. One car did stop, but only to avoid hitting a kid that had run into the street spitting out an ant.

Isabella had the **super-creative** idea of going down the street and throwing cups of lemonade at passing cars so they'd have to stop and get them washed, but most of the lemonaded cars just kept going. One lady got out and yelled and acted like she might chase Isabella, but it didn't happen. Adults often think chasing is a good idea until they actually have to do it.

Isabella was in a pretty bad mood after that. She walked down to Emmily's house because ordering somebody around always cheers her up, but Emmily wasn't home, so Isabella came back and tried ordering us around. **It didn't work.** We were too depressed. We just picked up our stuff and called it a day.

When I got home, my mom said she tried to take a look at our online auction but she couldn't get into the account, and she wondered if Isabella might have accidentally changed the password.

I'm sure she just typed it wrong, but I told her I'd ask Isabella tomorrow.

It's probably that the whole Internet thing is too **scientific** for my mom's old head. I've seen old people fumble with technology many, many times.

Friday 20

Dear Dumb Diary,

This morning, Margaret called me. You might remember, Dumb Diary, that Margaret is the pencil chewer who is generally nice but also partially gross. (I'm sorry, Margaret, but on a scale of one to ten, you're normally only a five. But when you chew, **both** you and your pencils are number twos.)

But let's not talk about Margaret anymore because it wasn't her on the phone at all. It was Isabella, doing one of her masterful **voice impersonations** to fool my mom.

Isabella can perfectly imitate the following voices:

1. Margaret
2. A crazy, angry old lady from Europe
3. A panic-stricken Elmo
4. A crazy, angry old lady from someplace near Europe

She cleverly chose to imitate Margaret this time, because people just hang up on her when she does the others.

Isabella wanted to work on the computer over at Emmily's house, but she wasn't home again this morning. I'm beginning to think that it's only a matter of time before we learn on the news that Emmily was abducted by headhunters — and then returned — because her head is **no prize**.

I asked Isabella to work over here, but she said my mom had called her mom last night to ask questions about our online auction and she really didn't want to get quizzed about it by my mom, too.

So I quizzed her.

Isabella said the auction is going fine and she really didn't need a bunch of ~~halfwits~~ (I'm sure she meant to say "people") breathing down her neck.

She said that if I left everything to her, we'd be just fine, and I shouldn't ask questions. Then she reminded me of times in the past when I'd asked questions and later wished I hadn't.

Just then, Isabella heard my mom in the background and said, "Quick! Say something that will make her think you're talking to Margaret!"

"Yes, Margaret," I said immediately. "Pencils are very delicious things to chew and you are chewing on one now, Margaret. And they're **vegetarian.**"

I heard Isabella's palm hit her forehead.

Look, we don't all have the brain chemical that helps us commit fraudulent acts. Sure, we might wish we did, but we don't.

Mom gave me the same suspicious look she gives my dad and Stinker when something in the room smells.

"Is that Isabella?" she asked.

"Margaret!" I laughed into the phone convincingly. "You'll never believe this, Margaret, but my mom thinks you're Isabella, Margaret."

My mom reached for the phone. "Let me say hello to Margaret again," she said.

"Good-bye-Margaret-I-have-to-go-and-play-outside-in-ten-minutes-near-those-bushes-behind-the-Ryans'-house!" I shouted as Mom pried the phone out of my hands and Isabella hung up.

Not bad, huh? Maybe I DO have that brain chemical.

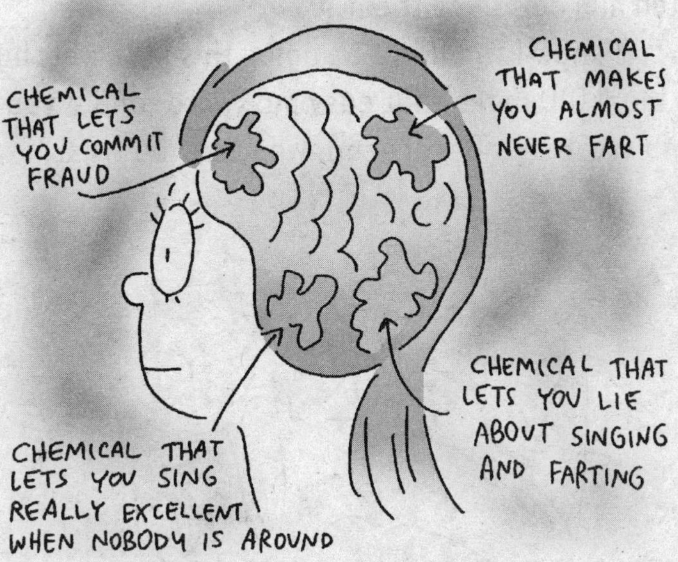

Isabella understood my clever code and showed up behind the Ryans' bushes ten minutes later. We talked quietly, which was weird because the Ryan triplets are usually screaming and howling, so you have to talk loudly when you're anywhere near their house just to hear each other.

Isabella said she needed to get on our computer and she didn't want a lot of questions about it. She said she knew exactly what she was doing, and if our moms would leave her alone, we'd be going to Screamotopia.

I told her that since tomorrow is Saturday, my dad would be busy doing no chores outside, and my mom would be in and out all morning trying to catch him not doing them.

I know I shouldn't be doing this in secret, but my mom DID make that easy password, and if you can't trust your best friend, who can you trust?

Saturday 21

Dear Dumb Diary,

Okay, well, maybe you can't trust anybody.

This morning, Isabella came over and my mom cornered her.

"Isabella, would you mind showing me the auction you're running?" she said.

"Sure, Mrs. Kelly," Isabella said, and started typing on the keyboard. There were the items, just like they were supposed to be.

"Doesn't look like anybody's bought anything yet," Isabella said directly to me. Then she glanced out the window. "Hey Jamie, **why is your dad sitting down out there?**"

That was all it took to make mom fly out the door. "He's **what???**"

Isabella started typing like mad as soon as she left. "Jamie, could you just, you know, please beat it?" And she jerked her thumb in the air to punctuate it.

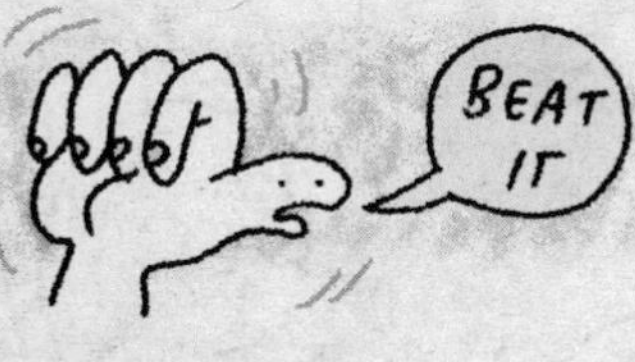

So I did. Isabella needed her space, and I gave it to her. I went upstairs and watched Stinker and Stinkette take turns wrecking one of my dad's socks. (Hey, here's a thought: Maybe we should manufacture **foot-flavored dog food.**)

Suddenly, the dogs' ears flipped up. I thought I heard it, too — the back door opening and closing very quietly.

I listened until the silence was interrupted by (in this order) Isabella screaming, somebody hitting a bag of flour with a baseball bat, my mom screaming something I couldn't quite get but it was possibly sweary, and my dad coming inside screaming about what all the screaming was about.

There was no baseball bat and there was no bag of flour. But there *was* my mom's stomach and Isabella's fist, and those were responsible for that particular sound.

The scream Isabella let out was because my mom snuck up on her and surprised her from behind. I could have told Mom that she was going to get punched for it — it's an instinct that Isabella can't help.

My mom's screaming was because of the punch (**Isabella punches great**), and because of what she saw on the computer screen.

Isabella had another eBay auction going — her own special auction. One that involved me and Angeline, without us even knowing it.

You know those pictures that Isabella took of us in matching black T-shirts? Turns out that they were **not** for a brochure advertising our business. They were to advertise a product that Isabella had **invented**.

It was called "Herb-tastical-abulous Vegetarian Beauty Lemonade" (I **KNEW** she liked my company names!!!), and Isabella was selling each treatment for $12.00. And she had orders — lots of 'em.

I was so happy that she had figured out a way to solve our money problem and get us to Screamotopia . . . until my mom and dad had to rain on the parade and point out that this stuff was totally fake, so it was illegal to sell — and not just a little bit illegal.

This is not one of those adorable crimes that Isabella commits sometimes. This is stuff that makes the news. It was lucky that Isabella had not accepted any of the payments yet and could just **cancel** all of the orders.

And then there was another sound, one where I sucked in so hard I thought I might suffocate.

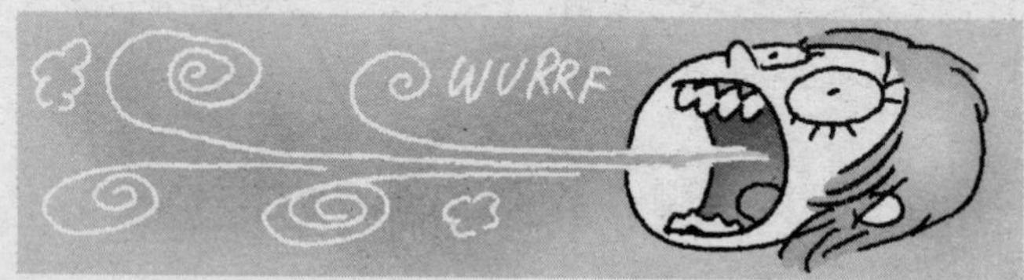

The pictures were "Before" and "After" pictures. **And I was the "Before."** That was why Isabella wanted me to cut my hair, so my hair length would match Angeline's. She didn't think anybody would believe it was the same person if the hair was ***that*** different.

"I can't believe you made me a 'Before' picture in a beauty ad!" I said.

Isabella just shrugged. "Look at the pictures, Jamie. Who would believe you were the 'After'?"

She might have been right, but this was a good example of why being right is **overrated**. Often it's best to avoid it.

Isabella's mom came and got her and led her out to the car. It reminded me of when you see them walking someone to the electric chair in movies. And now that I think about it, why do they even use a chair? So that you'll be **comfortable**? If they're so concerned about that, why don't they make it an electric couch?

I'm so mad at Isabella right now. Plus, I'm sad on top of it, because I don't see how we can possibly make enough money for Screamotopia in just six days. I'm not even sure I'd want to go with Isabella now anyway.

What could be worse?

Sunday 22

Dear Dumb Diary,

Aunt Carol came over today, and I told her how our moneymaking efforts were going. She's my aunt, so she politely made **faces of anger** when I told her what Isabella had done, because making **faces of anger** is something we do for the people we care about when they're angry. Also you're supposed to make **faces of surprise** when they tell you something that you know they think is surprising, even if it isn't. Making faces is the glue that holds civilization together.

Then Aunt Carol told me something that really *was* surprising, and I didn't even have to fake a face over it.

We're going to Screamotopia after all!!!!!!!!!

And it's all thanks to Angeline.

Aunt Carol wasn't supposed to tell me, but because I was so, so, so, so sad, she couldn't help herself. I can understand why: My fake sad face is almost impossible to deal with. My real sad face is just **excellently devastating**.

Angeline cut her hair off **to sell it**. I couldn't believe it. And when I asked Aunt Carol if she could possibly get $300.00, for it, she laughed and laughed.

She showed me a website that helps people sell their hair to wigmakers. Some people were getting almost ten times that much, and their hair was **nothing** compared to Angeline's!

I asked Aunt Carol how much Angeline got for her hair, but she didn't know. She wasn't even supposed to know any of it, but Uncle Dan heard about it and made her promise not to tell me.

Then she made **me** promise not to tell Isabella. But not the way she had promised Uncle Dan. Or the way Uncle Dan had promised Angeline's mom. She meant I had to **really** promise. A real real real real promise.

THE FOUR KNOWN KINDS OF PROMISES

A PROMISE

A PROMISE WITH AN EXPIRATION DATE. A PROMISE PEOPLE KEEP FOR A WHILE.

A REAL, REAL, REAL, REAL PROMISE

THIS IS THE ONE PROMISE YOU MUST NEVER BREAK.

A PINKY PROMISE

AUTOMATICALLY NOT A PROMISE BECAUSE TOUCHING PINKIES LIKE THIS IS SO DUMB.

A REAL REAL, REAL, REAL PROMISE.

OKAY, SOMETIMES THESE GET BROKEN BUT IT'S NOT YOUR FAULT SINCE YOU REALLY MEANT FOR IT NOT TO.

Monday 23

Dear Dumb Diary,

If you forget a promise, it shouldn't count.

I **ALMOST** told Isabella today. I talked to her on the phone first thing, and I forgot I was mad at her and forgot I promised and I came close to telling her about Angeline's hair sale.

"Maybe I shouldn't have used you as the 'Before' picture," Isabella said, which was the most heartfelt apology I'd ever heard her make. **See how nice she is?** I would have cried, except she would have made fun of me for it and that would have made me cry even more.

"It's okay. It doesn't matter. We're still going to Screamotopia," I said.

"Well, Jamie, I'm not sure tha — " She stopped herself in mid-sentence. "What makes you think so?" she said, and I could feel **suspiciousness rays** beaming out of the phone.

"Oh. Just because," I said. Then I winked, but I realized she couldn't hear that over the phone. "I just winked," I added.

I asked Isabella to come over, but she said her mom was still cranky because she did commit a little bit of a huge beauty-product-selling crime and she figured she's grounded for at least a day.

I couldn't call Angeline, because I would surely give it away that I knew that she had sold her hair so that we could all go to Screamotopia. Plus, I was grateful for her sacrifice, and I really didn't feel like being grateful to Angeline any sooner than I had to.

So I was on my own.

Since we're now wealthy, I really didn't have anything to do all day. I just **luxuriated uselessly.**

I set up a lounge chair in the backyard to drape myself over — a favorite rich-person activity — and brought out my iPod, a book, a lemonade, my sunglasses, some nail polish, some premium gum (that kind in the sophisticated package), and a bottle of mom's perfume to spray around because wealthy people do that, too.

I let Stinker and Stinkette play out in the yard, and I pretended that they were my priceless miniature Shetland ponies. Except Stinker, who is a Shetland hippopotamus.

I relaxed and stretched out glamorously, and enjoyed my book and lemonade and premium gum and everything, and after about 15 minutes of being fabulously wealthy, I was so bored I couldn't stand it.

And I came upon this wealth **for free**. Aren't the best things in life supposed to be free? They should be easier to enjoy.

Tuesday 24

Dear Dumb Diary,

Isabella came over today, and so did Angeline. I talked and talked about Screamotopia and neither Isabella or Angeline seemed very excited, which was weird.

"You know, Jamie," Isabella said, "unless you found a suitcase of money somewhere, I don't see any way we're going."

"Yeah," I said, "but you know. You **know**. *You* know, right, Angeline? I mean, right? ***You know.***" I started making discreet clippy motions with my fingers, and then cleverly rubbed them together to represent money.

A light came on in Angeline's eyes. "Oh. Yeah. I know what you're getting at," she said.

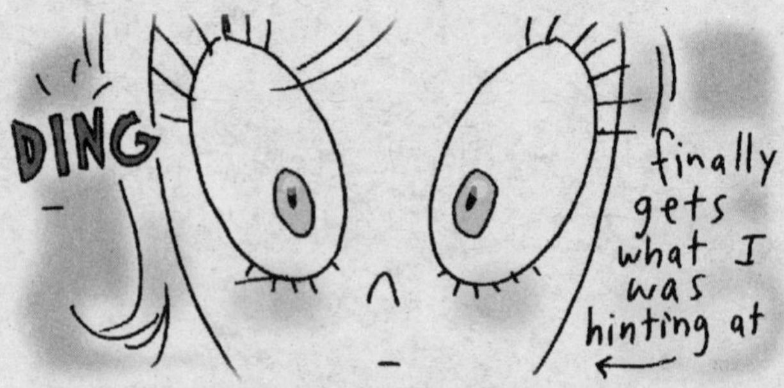

"ANGELINE CUT HER HAIR AND SOLD IT SO WE CAN GO TO SCREAMOTOPIA," I blurted out, not really breaking any promise because Angeline was about to say it anyway.

Isabella looked at Angeline's head. "Really? How much can you get for a head?" she asked. "I mean — you know — a head of hair."

"Hair like Angeline's goes for like three thousand bucks, I bet," I said. "Right, Angeline?"

Angeline smiled and nodded. "Yeah, it could go for that much," she said, but she looked kind of uncomfortable. I wondered if the sensation of being nice and nicely earning us money was unusual to her, and therefore a bit unsettling.

Isabella smiled. "Hmmmmmm," she said. "Well then, thanks, Angeline. Did you get the money yet?"

"No," Angeline said. Then she suggested we set up the lemonade stand again or wash cars or something, but we didn't see why we would need to.

We're all set now. **No problems.**

Wednesday 25

Dear Dumb Diary,

Angeline called today, and you are not going to believe how SELFISH she is, Dumb Diary: We're not getting *any* of her hair money to go to Screamotopia.

Because there isn't any.

At first I thought it might be because her hair doesn't look like it came from a human being, so the wigmakers might not want it.

But that wasn't it.

Angeline SELFISHLY donated her hair to charity.

She said that she *was* going to sell it, but her stylist told her about this charity for kids who are having medical treatments that make their hair fall out. They use donated hair to make wigs for the kids until their real hair grows back.

I asked Angeline why she didn't at least keep a pigtail for us so we could go to Screamotopia, but she said she couldn't bring herself to sell it after she heard about the kids.

Angeline said she took my hair that day and donated it as well. Which, when you think of it, is stealing, even though my mom had tossed it in the trash.

Then she said she'd see how much babysitting money she had, and maybe that would be enough for all of us to go to Screamotopia.

I was so mad I just **hung up** on her.

I called Isabella, and she wasn't very worried. She said that Angeline had given her an idea for another sale she had going, a very special sale that was going to make us all the money we needed.

See, Isabella almost never has just one plan. She says that any idiot can come up with a plan. If you **really** want to succeed, you have to have a plan B in case your first plan, like selling a fraudulent beauty product, doesn't work out.

This gave me an idea for another invention...

When you're **REALLY** mad at somebody...

Don't settle for disconnecting by just pressing a button...

HANG-UP HAMMER

GET THE NEW

HANG-UP HAMMER

And let them know how you feel!

I was so relieved that Isabella had this all under control. Nothing to worry about.

It's amazing, isn't it? How one second you think you're going to Screamotopia, then you think you aren't, then you think are again, then you think you aren't. Then you talk to your best friend and you know you are again. I wonder if Screamotopia has any roller coasters this nauseating.

Thursday 26

Dear Dumb Diary,

Angeline came over today and tried to talk me into one last attempt at making the money we need.

"No worries," I told her. "Isabella has us covered."

Then Isabella's mom showed up with Isabella and sat her right down on the couch.

"Tell them," she said.

"You're not allowed to sell human heads," Isabella said. "And I did and the police came and now I don't have the money we need. Can we go now?"

Her mom explained it a little better. Isabella sold a shrunken head to her mean older brothers for **THREE HUNDRED DOLLARS**, and they turned around and sold it to another kid whose dad is a policeman.

Have you ever seen a shrunken head, Dumb Diary? It's one of those little horrible heads you see in scary movies. They're all gross and withered and look like an *old rotten peach* . . . which Isabella admitted this was.

I was so moved.

"Isabella," I said. "You *loved* that peach. And you were willing to sacrifice it for us?"

Isabella's mom answered for her. "She carved it up a little, stuffed the mouth full of her old baby teeth, attached some hair to it, and tricked her brothers into buying it." She didn't seem to be as moved as I was, for some reason.

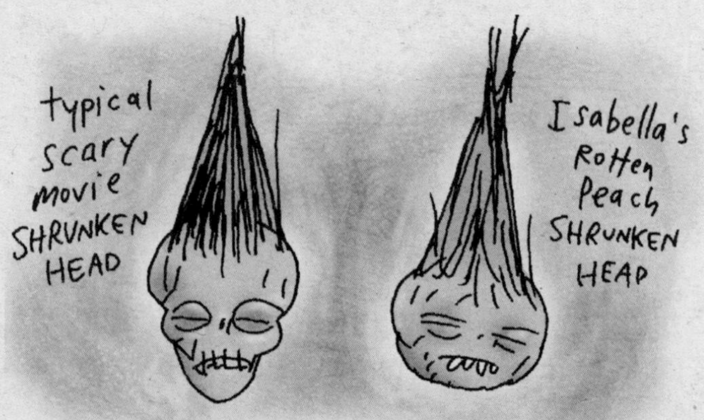

I asked Isabella where she got the hair, but she didn't want to talk about that.

Isabella's mom explained what had happened. "The kid they sold the peach to showed it to his dad, the cop, who instantly realized that it wasn't a shrunken head. His son had been swindled, so he came over to our house to get the money back and have a talk with Isabella and her brothers."

"He remembered me," Isabella said. "He was the one that came when I did my disease report. He put me in handcuffs."

"He did not, Isabella," her mom snapped. "And she would have been in a **lot** more trouble, except she reminded the policeman that since his son bought it *thinking* it was a real head, he would be in trouble, too," Isabella's mom added.

Isabella smiled slightly.

But her mom was not smiling. "Promise me you won't sell human body parts anymore, Isabella."

"You never let me do anything," Isabella said. Of course, I **agreed** with her. "Besides, it wasn't even real," she added.

Then Isabella's mom got a little louder and started talking about how if one more policeman showed up it would give her a heart attack and all that stuff.

Finally, Isabella yelled "**OKAY!**" which is really the only way to make a mom stop yelling. I've even seen my dad do it.

So that looks like the end, Dumb Diary. No money means no amusement park.

We were so close. We all tried. We tried everything we could think of. Angeline even tried to sell her beloved hair, but her **goodness** stopped her.

Isabella tried to sell her beloved peach, but **federal law** stopped her.

I know they say the best things in life are free, but it seems to me that the worst things in life are **also** free.

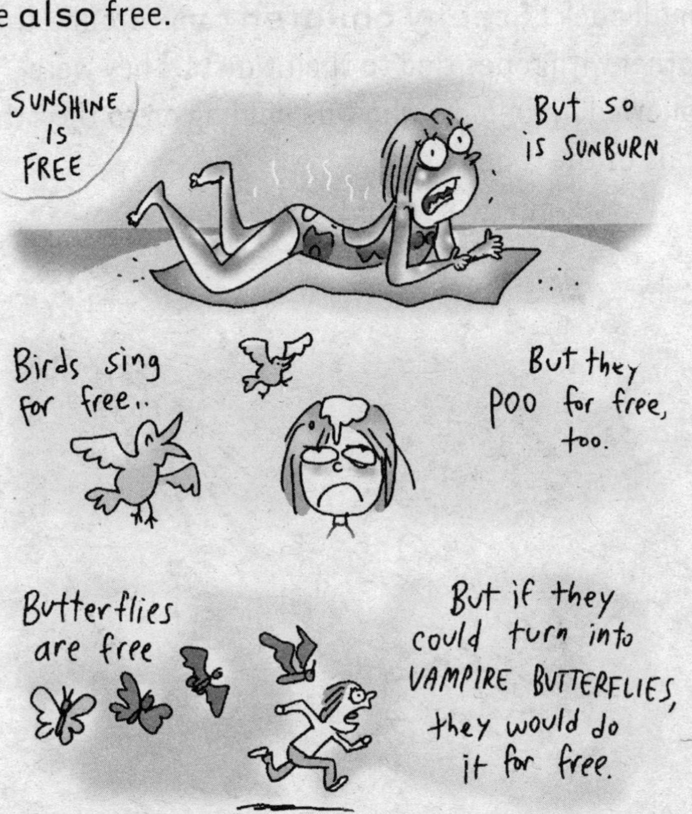

Friday 27

Dear Dumb Diary,

Angeline and Isabella came over for lunch today. I didn't want to tell Aunt Carol and Uncle Dan all by myself that we had bombed out. We sat out front and tried to figure out what to say, when a small pack of teeny children came around the corner with ropes tied to their waists. They were followed by Emmily, who was holding on to the other ends of the ropes.

"Hi, guys," she said.

"What are you doing to those kids?" Angeline asked.

"I'm walking them," Emmily said, "like I've been doing all week. I just walk them up and down the street. You know, for your business."

She explained that last week, when she was walking Cigarette Grandson, Mrs. Ryan saw her out the window and asked her to walk the triplets, too, probably just to get a minute's peace. Then another mom saw them and asked her to walk her son. They've all been paying her **a dollar per kid per hour**. I'm not even sure it's legal to walk kids like that.

"I have to get Joey home right away for his lunch," Emmily said. She headed down the street, and we followed along behind her.

She walked Joey up to the door and he ran up to Cigarette Lady, laughing. I guess he loved being walked. The Ryan triplets were happy, too. Maybe they were just **screamy** all the time because they wanted to go outside.

"Thank you, Emmily," Cigarette Lady wheezed, waving at us.

"You're welcome, Cigarette Lady," Emmily called back to her.

That's when we saw Aunt Carol and Uncle Dan pull up in my driveway. We told Emmily to meet us at my house after she dropped off the rest of the kids.

We told Aunt Carol and Uncle Dan the horrendously bad news, every single bit of it, from the lemonade stand to Emmily's baby-walking service. And Aunt Carol rubbed our short haircuts and said she might like to get hers cut, too, which seemed beside the point to me.

When we were done, they both stood up and said maybe we could try again next summer.

Then my mom came in holding the phone. She said my dad had told her to go check the auction, because it looked like somebody had bought our disgusting junk for **two hundred dollars**.

It was a **SCREAMOTOPIA MIRACLE**!

We started jumping up and down and laughing and I saw my mom shaking her head. There was something about how she shook it that made me wonder for a second if my dad had been the one that bought all the stuff.

When Emmily knocked on the door we were all still laughing, because it actually seemed possible that we might really make it to Screamotopia after all.

"Before I forget," Emmily said, "here's your money." And she handed me just under **a hundred dollars.**

"You made all this?" I said. Added to the auction money, and the $5.50 it took us all month to earn, **it was enough.**

Emmily was so truly happy for us that her genuine sweet smile was like a **cheery pink chainsaw** cutting me in half with guilt. Only Emmily, hardworking Emmily, had made any real money this summer.

"So this is the baby walker," Aunt Carol said. "I don't suppose you'd be willing to walk us all around Screamotopia?"

"Emmily can go?" Angeline, Isabella, and I all said at the same time. (It hurt my brain a little that Angeline and I would ever say anything at the same time, but I tried to look past it.)

"She worked as hard as you three. Maybe harder," Uncle Dan said. "If her parents say it's okay, sure, she can go. We'll cover the extra cost."

Emmily smiled and clapped and laughed and laughed. And laughed. And laughed. "Go where?" she finally asked.

Oh, Emmily.

I explained it all to her, which is why now I'm too tired to write another word. I have to get up early tomorrow morning for **SCREAMOTOPIA!!** Good night!

Saturday 28

Dear Dumb Diary,

I only have a minute to write, because I SLEPT IN.

I know, right?

I was supposed to be up early, and now everybody (including Emmily) is on their way over right this minute to pick me up to head to SCREAMOTOPIA!!!

It's going to be a blast. And honestly, for a boring, stupid month of trouble, in a weird way it's been sort of fun.

I think I may understand how the best things in life can be free, even though the worst things are also free. Screamotopia is going to be great, and it's really expensive. But other really expensive things, like fake shrunken heads, can be worthless.

You know, I don't think you can tell how much something is worth by how much it costs.

Maybe that saying should just go, **"The best things in life are."**

Thanks for listening, Dumb Diary,

Jamie Kelly

P.S. They just pulled up, but one more thing: When we get back next week, we're all going to the zoo. Even Isabella. Remember when Angeline said she donated my hair? She never said where it went, until yesterday.

And now there's a warthog named Loverboy who doesn't mind the sun anymore, thanks to a new artificial mane that somebody donated to him. **FOR FREE.**

Thinking of cutting your hair?

Don't forget to ask your parents first! They might be able to help you get involved with Locks of Love, Wigs for Kids, or the Childhood Leukemia Foundation, organizations that make wigs for kids in need.

If you want to donate your hair to a warthog, you're on your own.

CHECK OUT ALL OF JAMIE KELLY'S DEAR DUMB DIARY BOOKS!

WWW.SCHOLASTIC.COM/DEARDUMBDIARY